THE AMAZING AMOS

AND THE
GREATEST COUCH
ON EARTH

by SUSAN SELIGSON
and HOWIE SCHNEIDER

Joy Street Books
Little, Brown and Company
Boston Toronto London

To Jack, the best friend
a ''moose'' ever had

A Floyd Yearout Book

316 Wellesley Street, Weston, Massachusetts 02193

First Edition

Library of Congress Catalog Card Number 88-82601

Joy Street Books are published
by Little, Brown and Company (Inc.)

10 9 8 7 6 5 4 3 2 1

Published simultaneously in Canada
by Little, Brown & Company (Canada) Limited

Printed in Italy

Amos is an old dog who lives with Mr. and Mrs. Bobson.
Like most old dogs, Amos spends nearly
all his time on the couch.

But this is no ordinary couch.
With just a flick of his paw,
Amos can make his couch
MOVE!

VAROOM

Amos loves to ride his couch through town.
Mr. and Mrs. Bobson don't
worry about him.

They know he's a good driver.

He is always home in time for dinner . . .

and for his favorite games.

One morning, Amos set out for the park as usual.

He said hello to all his friends along the way.

But this morning, when he got to the park, things looked different.

Amos had never seen
such a peculiar crowd.

And they had never seen a dog drive a couch.

"Hey . . . Amos, we're just about to break for lunch," Knocko the clown announced. "Care to join us?"

Amos was beginning to feel right at home.

But before he knew it, Knocko declared, "Lunch is over, my friends. Time to get back to work."

Then Felix the bear, Woody the monkey, and Knocko began to perform some of their stunts.

It looked like so much fun . . .
Amos decided to try
a few stunts, too.

First he juggled his cushions.

Next he spun on his wheels.

Then he glided through the hoop.

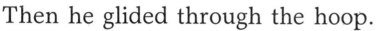

Finally he
spotted the ramp.

FULL SPEED AHEAD!

"Oh, dear," said Knocko.

"Don't feel bad. No one gets it right the first time."

"Come back tomorrow and you can try it again!"

"Did you have a nice day?" the Bobsons asked. "We cooked you your favorite supper — chicken!"

But Amos was too full and too tired to eat.

Soon he was fast asleep.

All night long Amos dreamed about his new friends.

Early the next morning, he was off.

VAROOM

When Amos got to the park, everybody was busy practicing.

"Amos! You're back!" said Knocko.
"Want to give the ramp another try?"

Amos
revved up
his couch . . .

but he still needed a little more practice.

THUNK

"You're getting closer," said Knocko.
"We know you can do it.
We'll try again tomorrow."

For the second day in a row, Amos was late heading home.

"Where does he go all day? He's going to wear himself out," said Mrs. Bobson. "He hasn't touched his food. I wonder if he's getting sick."

The Bobsons tried to entertain Amos.

But his old games seemed rather dull these days.

The next day the Bobsons were going out.
"We'll be back later," Mrs. Bobson said.
"Why don't you stay home and rest?
Have a good long nap."

Amos felt miserable.

"This is terrible," he thought.

"How will I see my friends?"
Amos wondered.

He tried to sleep.

But he was
wide awake.

"I can sneak out and be back in a few hours,"
Amos decided. "The Bobsons will never know."

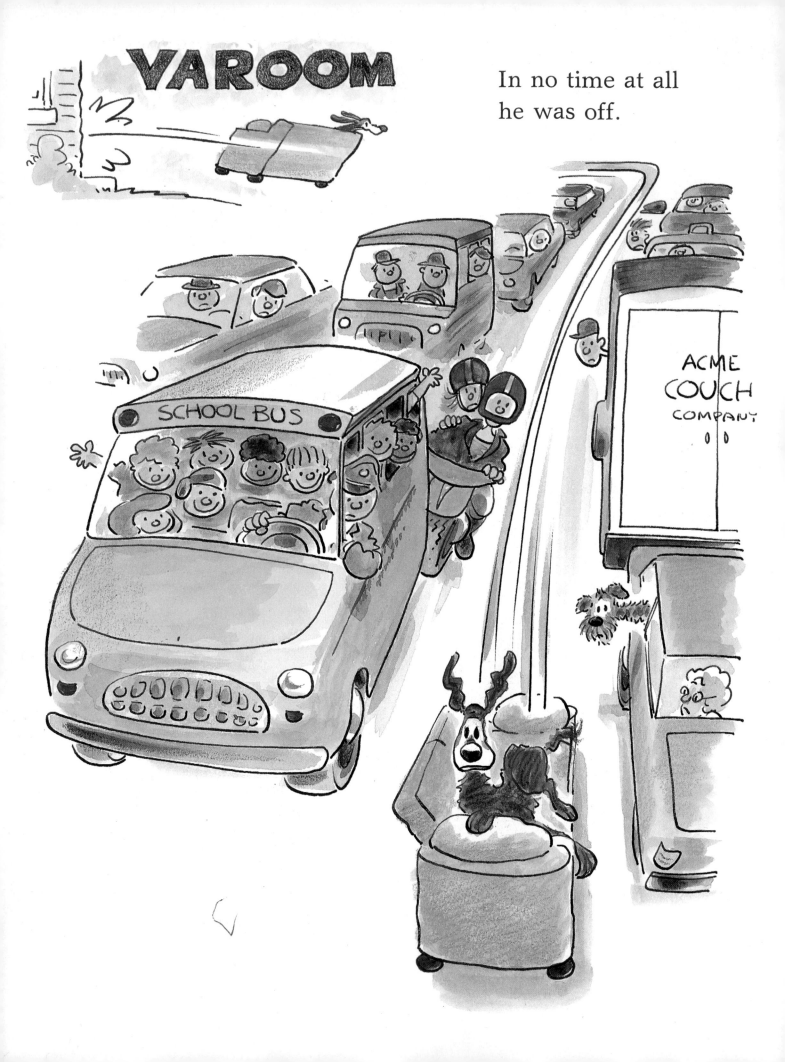

VAROOM

In no time at all
he was off.

"Where is everybody?"
Amos wondered.

"Hey, where do you think you're going?" the manager shouted. "We've got a show going on!"

NO DOGS ALLOWED

SCRAM

Suddenly Amos spotted Knocko.

HEY!

"What's going on here?" Amos wondered.

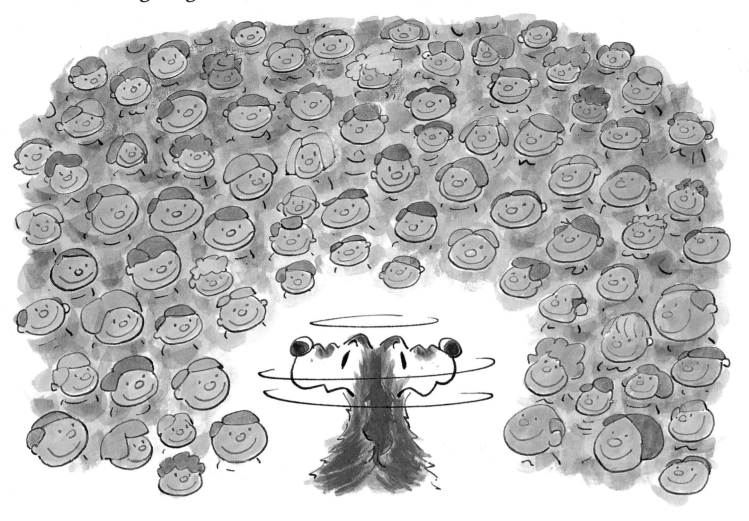

But he didn't have long to think about it.

"AMOS!"

"It's Amos!" Knocko cried.

But this was no time for a chat.

"It's Amos!" cried
another familiar voice.

And, just for a second, Amos took
his eyes off where he was going.

"So THIS is why you've been so tired,"
said Mr. Bobson.

"What an act!" said Knocko. "The Amazing Amos and the Greatest Couch on Earth!"

"Come on, circus star," said Mrs. Bobson.
"Time to head home."

And so they did.